THE PIRATE-CRUNCHER

Lubbers' Land

St. Andrew

St. David

The

Clarendon

Inner Harbour

Port Royal

Bull Bay

Galleon Harbour

Cow Bay

Half Moon Bay

Scurvy Sands

Cutlass Point

Fiddle Bay

Monkey Bay

Wreck Bay

Crunchy Head

Blubber Bay

Varmint's Head

Fish Head

Groody Head

Peak Bay

There Be
TREASURE
Abroad!

oooOoo-AaaARR!

Ye Wavy Bit...

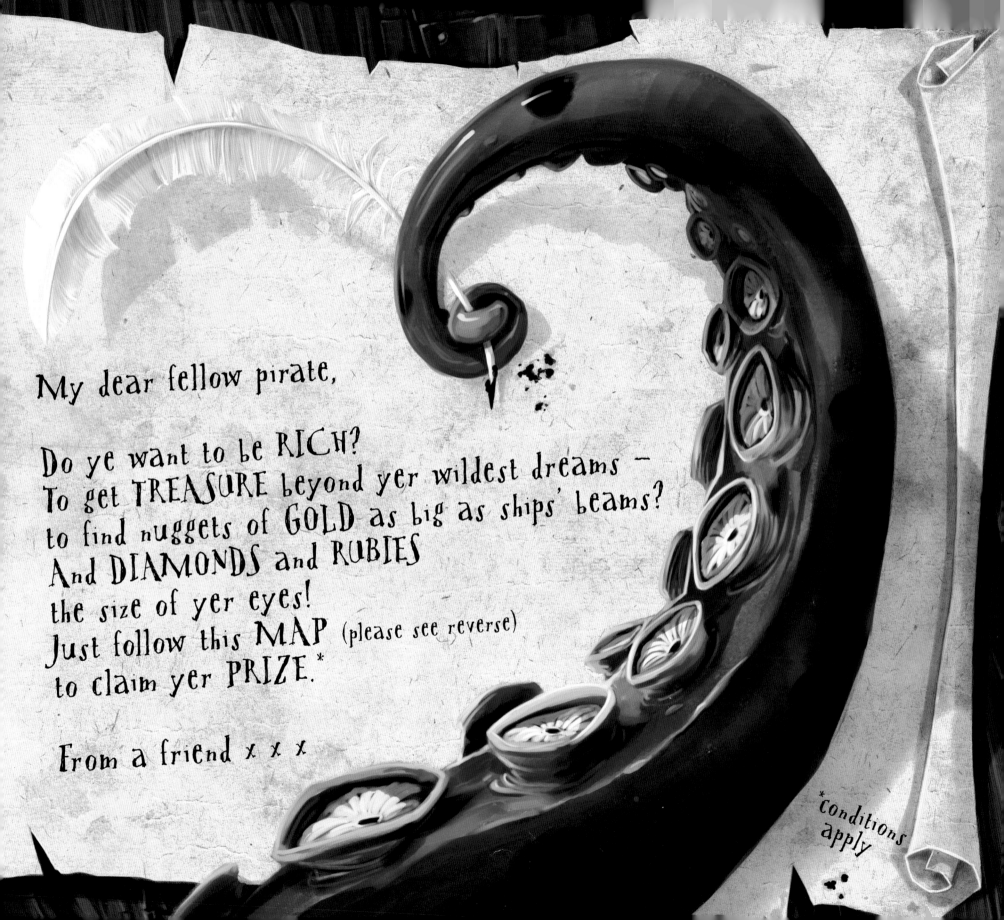

My dear fellow pirate,

Do ye want to be RICH?
To get TREASURE beyond yer wildest dreams –
to find nuggets of GOLD as big as ships' beams?
And DIAMONDS and RUBIES
the size of yer eyes!
Just follow this MAP (please see reverse)
to claim yer PRIZE.*

From a friend x x x

*conditions apply

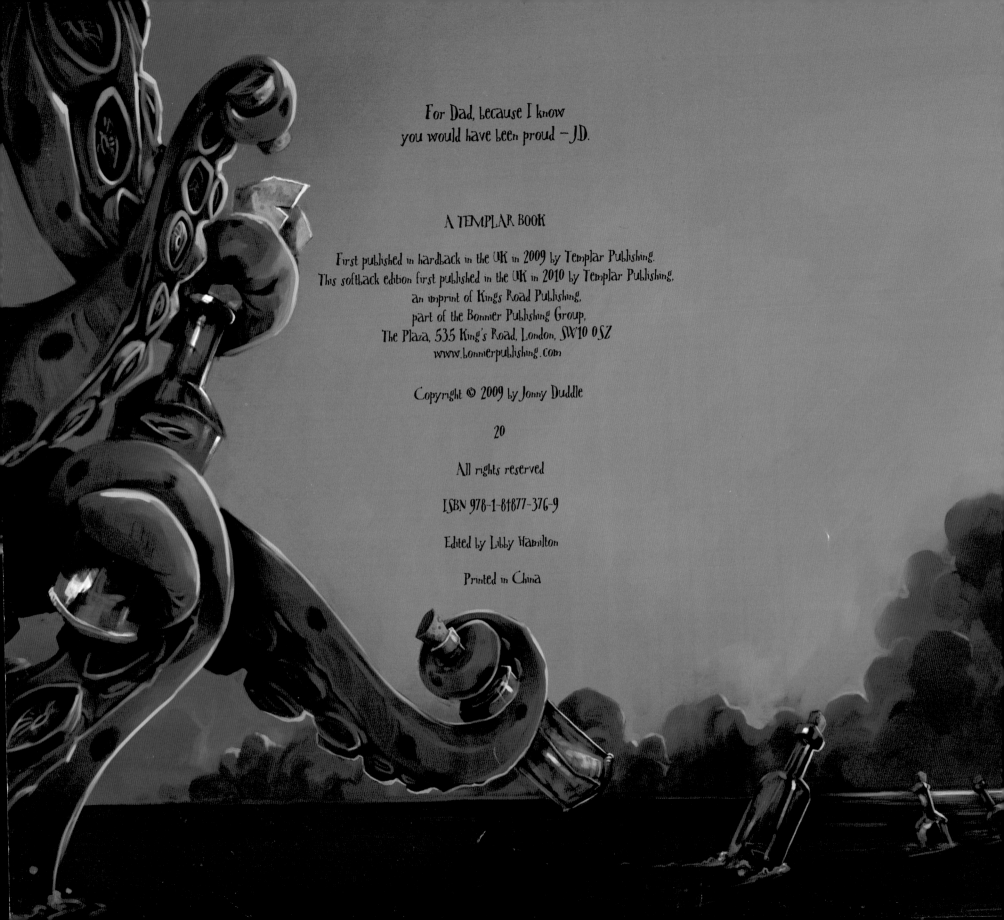

For Dad, because I know
you would have been proud – J.D.

A TEMPLAR BOOK

First published in hardback in the UK in 2009 by Templar Publishing.
This softback edition first published in the UK in 2010 by Templar Publishing,
an imprint of Kings Road Publishing,
part of the Bonnier Publishing Group,
The Plaza, 535 King's Road, London, SW10 0SZ
www.bonnierpublishing.com

Copyright © 2009 by Jonny Duddle

20

ISBN 978-1-84877-376-9

Edited by Libby Hamilton

Printed in China

THE PIRATE-CRUNCHER

JONNY DUDDLE

All was unusually quiet in Port Royal...

but if you listened carefully, on the quayside,

Thirsty
Parrot

you could hear the
faint sound of a fiddle
floating on the wind.

down the alleyways
and in the candlelit taverns,

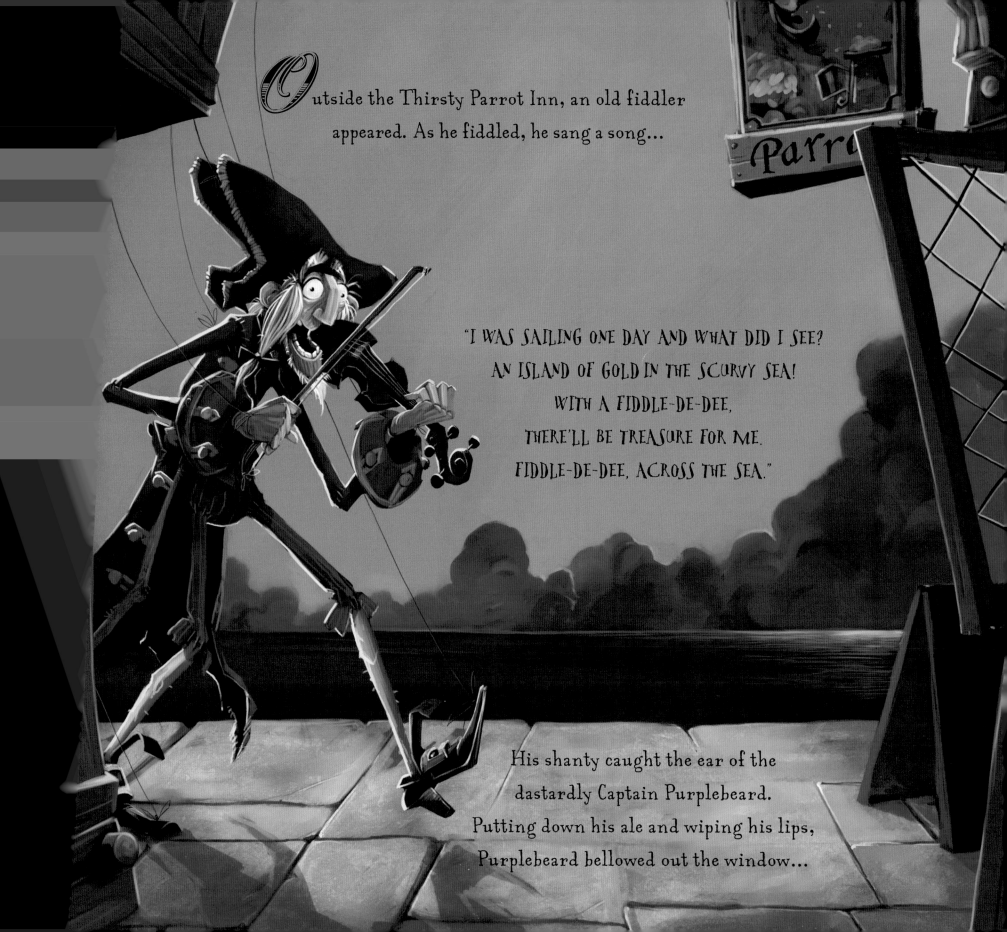

Outside the Thirsty Parrot Inn, an old fiddler appeared. As he fiddled, he sang a song...

"I WAS SAILING ONE DAY AND WHAT DID I SEE?
AN ISLAND OF GOLD IN THE SCURVY SEA!
WITH A FIDDLE-DE-DEE,
THERE'LL BE TREASURE FOR ME.
FIDDLE-DE-DEE, ACROSS THE SEA."

His shanty caught the ear of the dastardly Captain Purplebeard. Putting down his ale and wiping his lips, Purplebeard bellowed out the window...

To the Captain's delight the fiddler replied:

"AS I SAILED THE SEAS, I SCRIBBLED A MAP
SO THAT WHEN I GOT HOME I COULD FIND MY WAY BACK.
YE CANNOT IMAGINE THE BOOTY THAT'S THERE –
A HUGE HAUL OF TREASURE,
BEYOND COMPARE!"

Ha-HaRRR!

"I can imagine a SHIPLOAD of treasure," roared Captain Purplebeard.
"Diamonds and rubies and gold beyond measure..."

The fiddler unfurled
his map and sang:

"I'LL SHOW YE MY MAP IF YE'LL TAKE ME THERE –
THERE'LL BE TREASURE ENOUGH
FOR US ALL TO SHARE!"

The sun was coming up as Captain Purplebeard and his cut-throat crew boarded their ship, the BLACKHOLE. Behind them came the old fiddler, still dancing and singing:

"TO FIND THIS ISLAND, YOU'LL HAVE TO BE QUICK – FOR THEY SAY IT PERFORMS A VANISHING TRICK! AND NONE WHO'VE TRIED TO SET FOOT ON ITS SANDS, HAVE EVER RETURNED TO PIRATE LANDS."

But the Captain just sneered, "What NONSENSE, I say."

So off they sailed across the sea. And as they tucked into breakfast, the old fiddler began again:

"THERE IS ONE SMALL THING I FORGOT YESTERDAY –
THERE'S ALSO A MONSTER, OR SO THEY SAY.
HE LIKES TO EAT PIRATES WHO COME FOR HIS TREASURE,
AND HE CHEWS UP THEIR SHIPS,
JUST FOR GOOD MEASURE."

"YOU SCURVY SEA DOG!" bellowed the Captain.
"Be it MADE-UP or MONSTROUS, it's no match for me.

I'm Captain Purplebeard.

SCOURGE of the SEA!"

And the fiddler said:

"OH YES, I AGREE,
HE DOESN'T **SCARE** ME!

THOUGH, NO BONES ABOUT IT,
HE'S A **BIG** OLD BEAST,

WHO LIKES NOTHING MORE
THAN A PIRATE FEAST.

HE CAN SWALLOW WHOLE SHIPS
IN HIS WHIRLPOOL JAWS
(THOUGH THEY SAY HE'S ALLERGIC
TO SCARLET MACAWS)."

"THERE ARE RUBIES AND DIAMONDS
THE SIZE OF BALLOONS –
SILVER AND GUINEAS
AND GOLDEN DOUBLOONS.
BUT GRAB IT ALL QUICK
OR HE'LL HAVE YOUR ENTRAILS!
NOW, FIDDLE-DE-DEE, LET'S
SPREAD THOSE SAILS."

But no one moved
on the deck below.
The crew looked
around in FEAR
and DREAD,
as visions of
monsters filled
their heads...

"GO HOME?!" roared Captain Purplebeard. "I'll keelhaul you all, you cowardly landlubbers. The ONLY thing YOU need to be frightened of is ME!"

So with visions of monsters in EVERY head,
the motley old crew trudged off to bed.
Most had nightmares and TERRIBLE dreams
and the hold was full of pirate SCREAMS.

But up on the poop deck the captain was HAPPY,
for HIS head was full of dreams about treasure...
"GOLD or SILVER, I don't care which,
just as long as it makes me filthy RICH!"

Next morning, the crew were worried.
They couldn't be sure, but the day before
it seemed that they had numbered more...

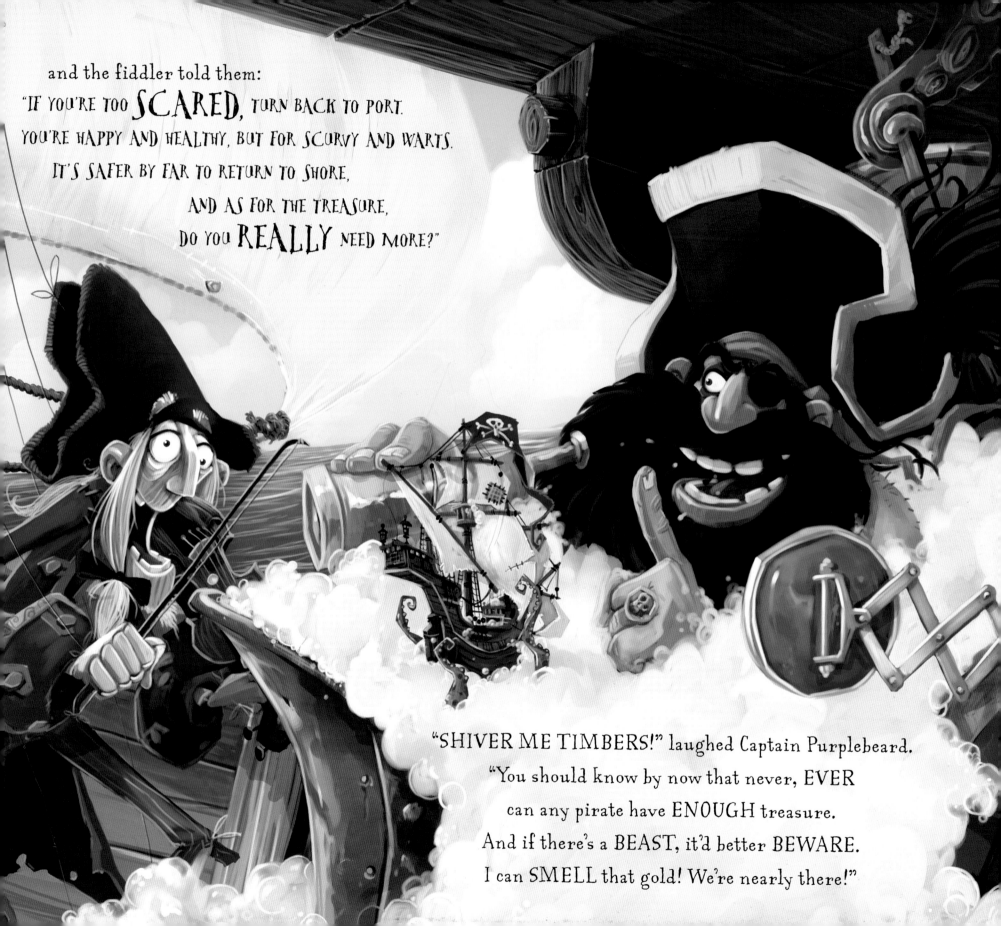

and the fiddler told them:
"IF YOU'RE TOO SCARED, TURN BACK TO PORT.
YOU'RE HAPPY AND HEALTHY, BUT FOR SCURVY AND WARTS.
IT'S SAFER BY FAR TO RETURN TO SHORE,
AND AS FOR THE TREASURE,
DO YOU REALLY NEED MORE?"

"SHIVER ME TIMBERS!" laughed Captain Purplebeard.
"You should know by now that never, EVER
can any pirate have ENOUGH treasure.
And if there's a BEAST, it'd better BEWARE.
I can SMELL that gold! We're nearly there!"

"HURRAH!" yelled the pirates, forgetting their fear, now the promise of treasure was so VERY near.

As they clambered ashore,
no one saw a thing wrong –
too busy to heed
the fiddler's
last song...

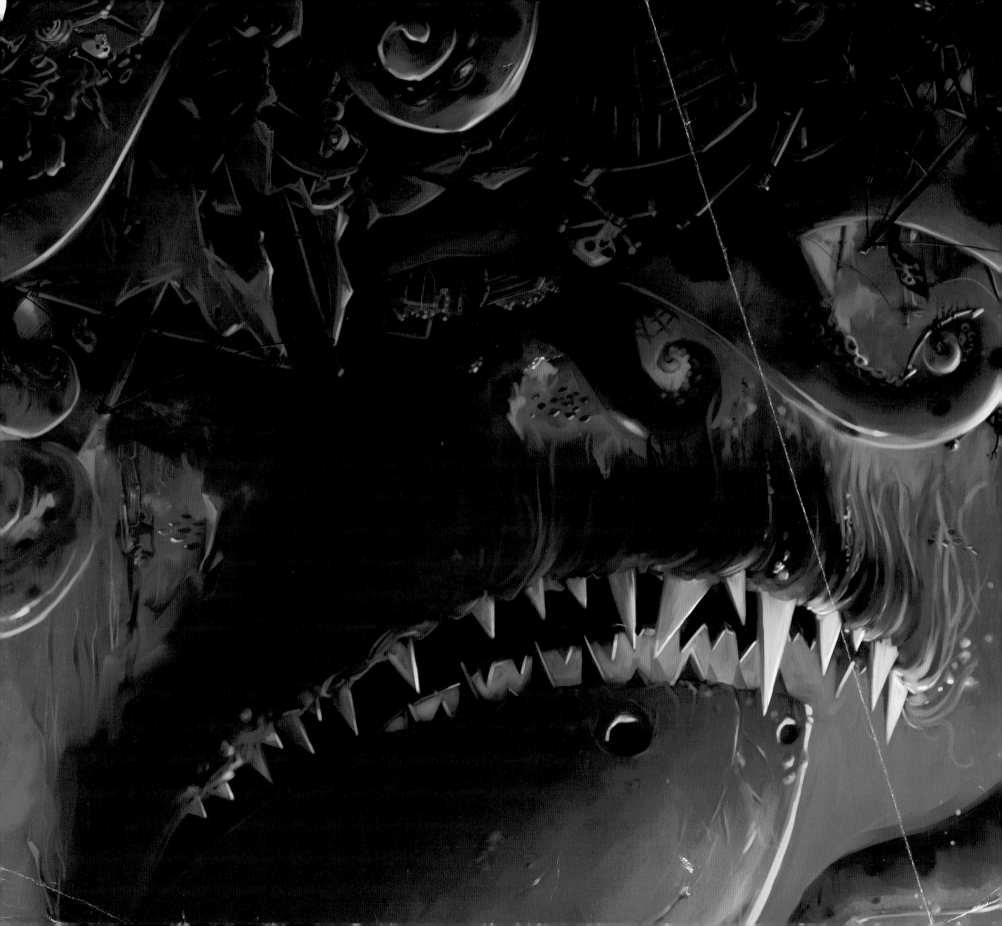

Lubbers' Land

St. Andrew

The B

St. David

Clarendon

Inner
Harbour

Port Royal

Bull Bay

Cow Bay

Cutlass Point

Fiddle Bay

Grindly Head

Mermaid's Head

Galleon Harbour

Half Moon Bay

Monkey Bay

Scurvy Sands

Wreck Bay

Butler Bay

Fish Head

Grozzly Head

Peak Bay

There Be
TREASURE
Abroad!

oooOoo-AaaARR!

Ye Wavy Bit...

A salty cove, Jonny Duddle
overheard the story of his first book,
THE PIRATE-CRUNCHER, while sailing in a square-rigger.
Then, in a quiet seaside town, he found an even stranger tale,
THE PIRATES NEXT DOOR, which has won the Waterstones
Children's Book Prize and become a best-seller.

Now in danger of becoming a landlubber,
Jonny lives in Wales with his wife Jane and
their daughters, Daisy and Rosie.